WELCOME to the fascinating world of origami! Here are some tips to keep in mind while folding:

- Pay careful attention to the dotted lines and arrows showing you which way to fold the paper.
- Always make sharp creases, using your fingernail, the bowl of a spoon, or a ruler to help smooth the folds.
- Keep a supply of scrap paper handy to practice making an object. Feel free to label your paper to match the diagrams.
- When following each step, it helps to look at the next diagram to see what the result should look like.
- When making a fold with tapered points, start at the narrowest portion of the point and then crease upward or outward from there.

Have fun folding!

Origami Symbols Key

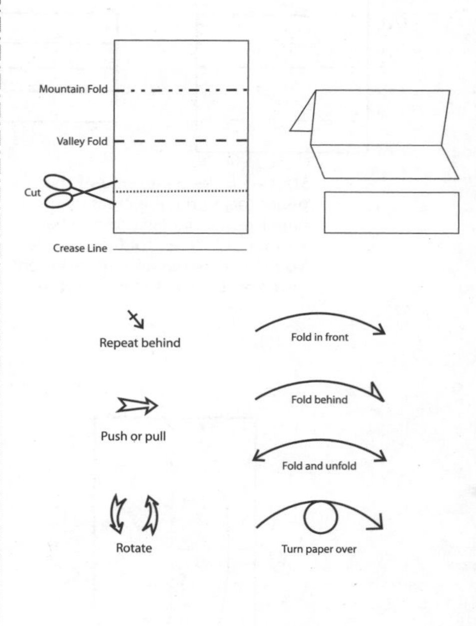

Butterfly

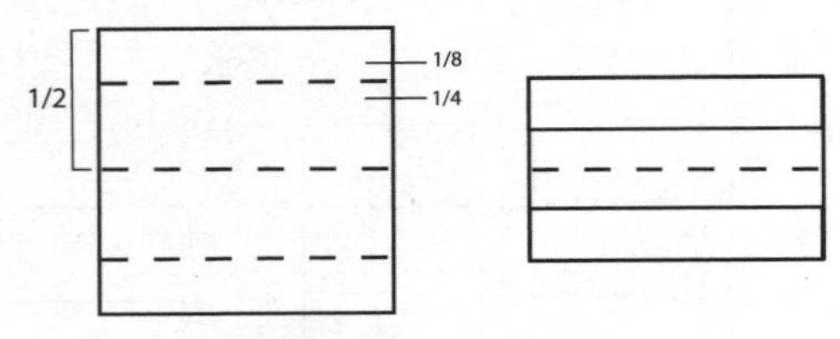

1. Start with the white side of the paper facing up. Pre-crease your paper as shown: First fold in half and unfold. Then, fold in the sides. You may experiment with different distances from the center crease.

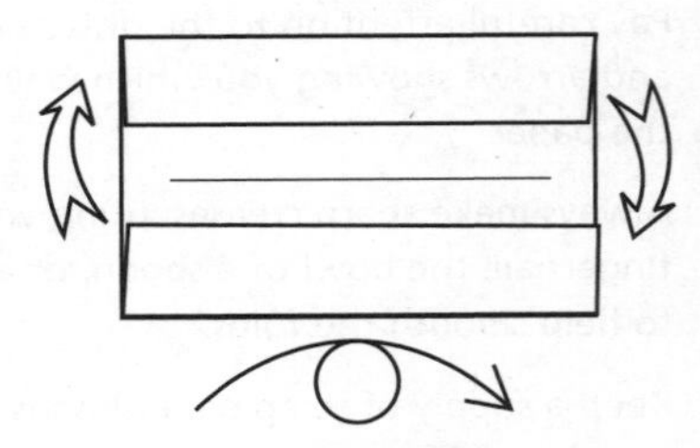

2. Rotate the paper 90°. Turn the paper over.

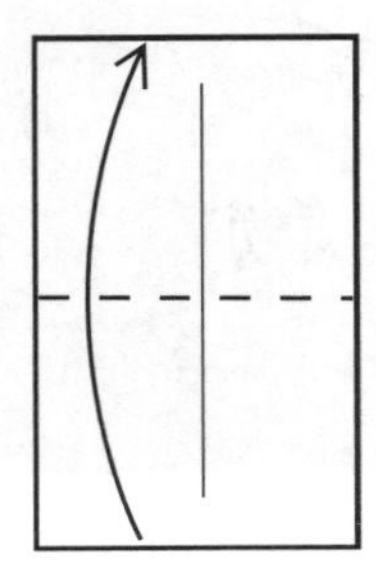

3. Fold in half, short edge to short edge.

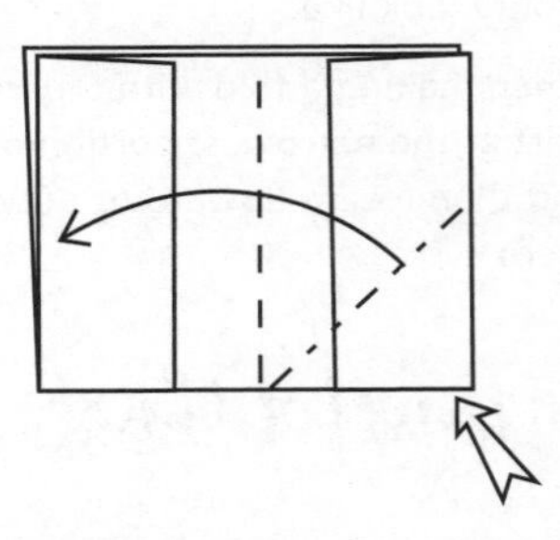

4. Move the top layer of the right half over to the left and flatten the paper. This is called a "squash fold."

Butterfly

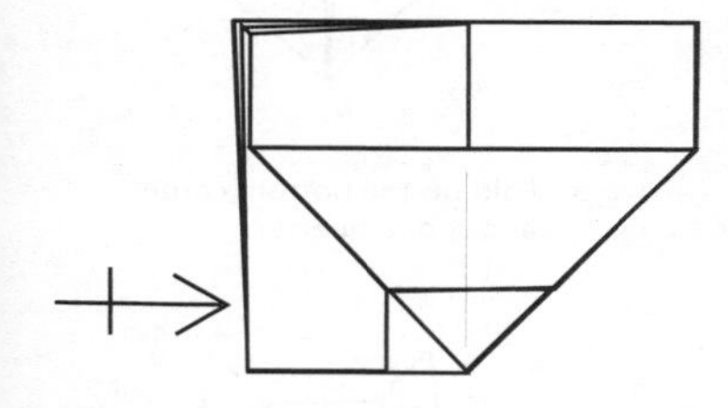

5. Squash fold the other side (behind) to match.

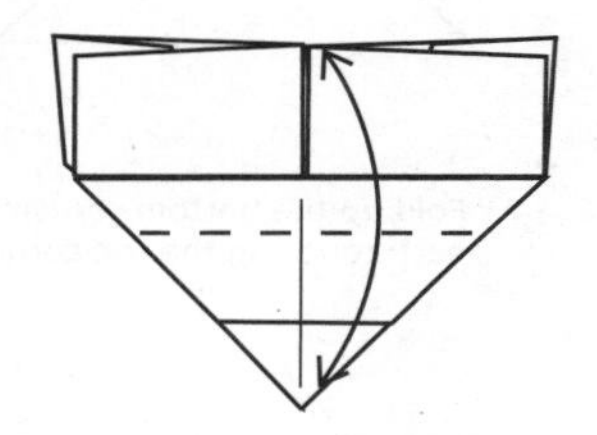

6. Fold up the bottom corner to the middle of the top edge and bring it back down.

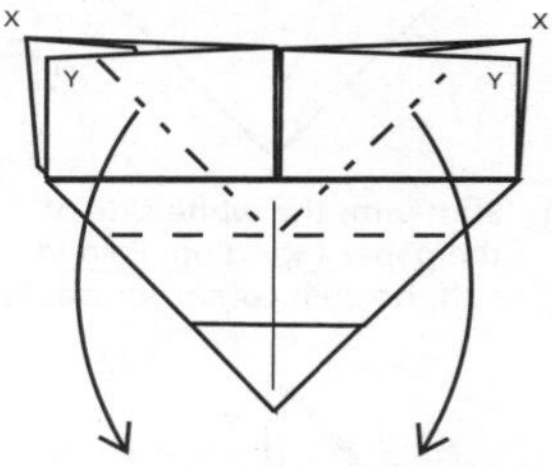

7. One at a time, squash-fold the left and right halves of the paper.

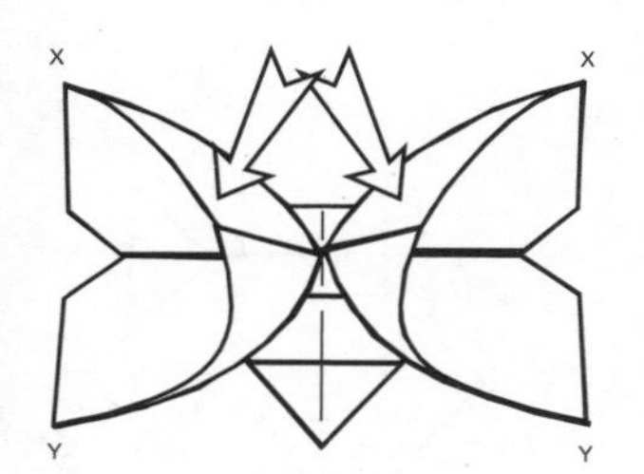

8. Squash fold in progress. Watch the "X" and "Y" corners.

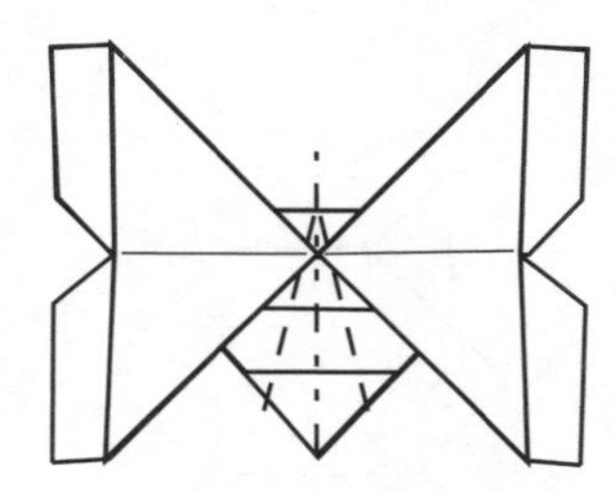

9. Mountain- and valley-fold the middle to form a body.

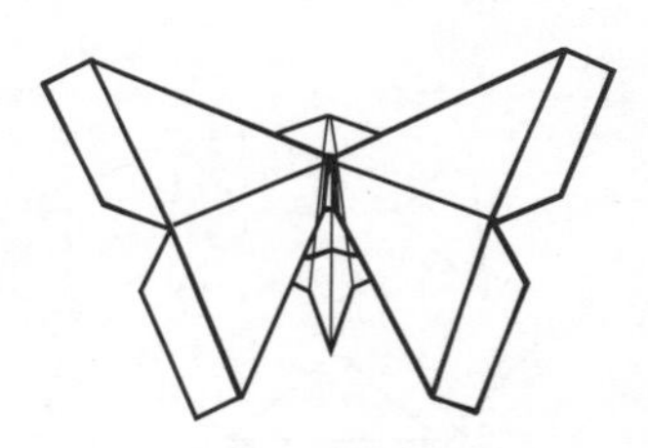

10. The finished Butterfly.

Cat Head

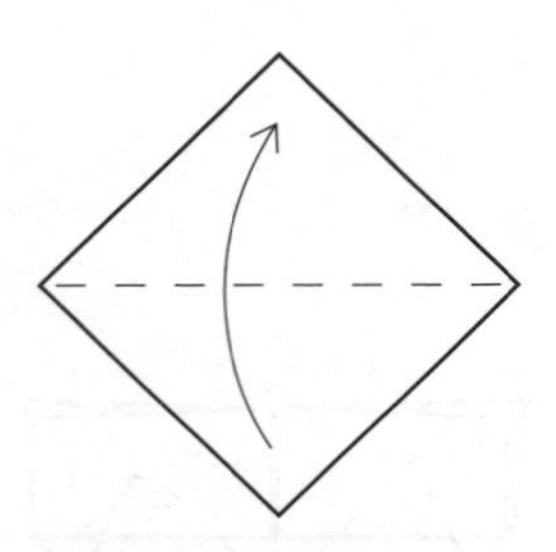

1. Start with the white side of the paper facing up. Fold in half, bottom corner to top.

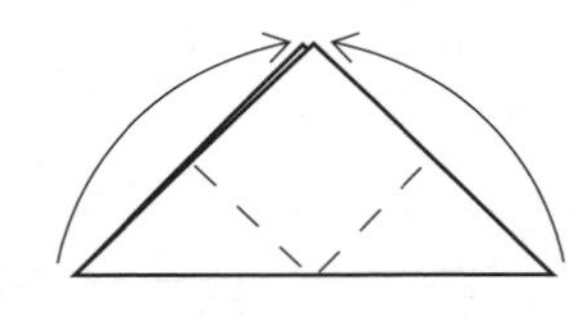

2. Fold up the bottom corners, each touching the top corner.

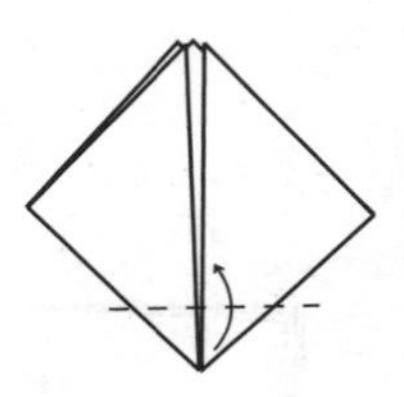

3. Fold up the bottom corner, about one quarter.

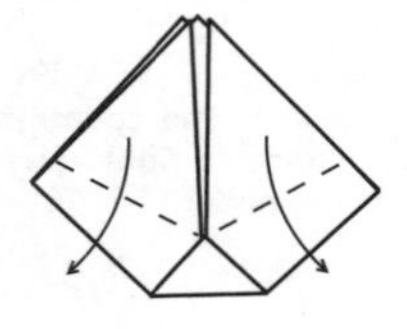

4. Fold down the top corners, matching their folded edges to the outline of the bottom triangle.

5. Turn over, top to bottom.

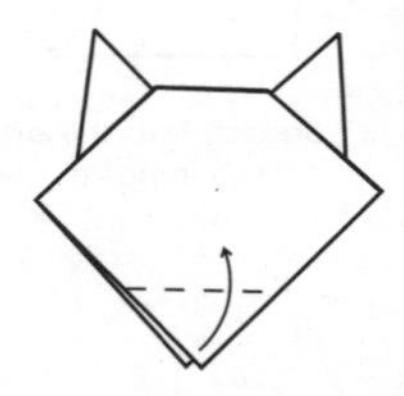

6. Fold up the bottom corner of the first layer.

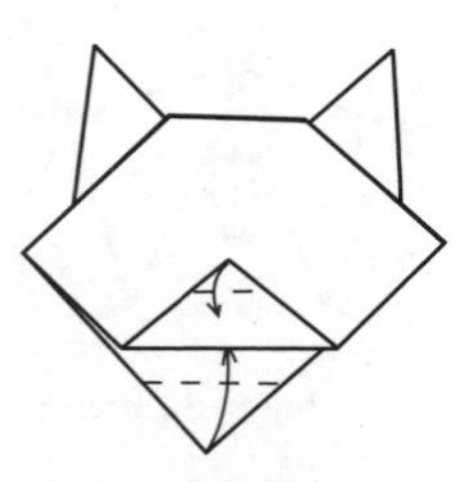

7. Fold up the bottom corner, tucking some of it under the folded edge. Fold down the top corner for a nose.

8. Mountain-fold the corners of the upper mouth under.

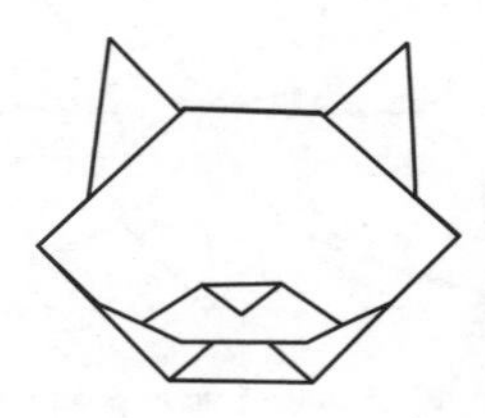

9. The finished Cat Head.

Bat

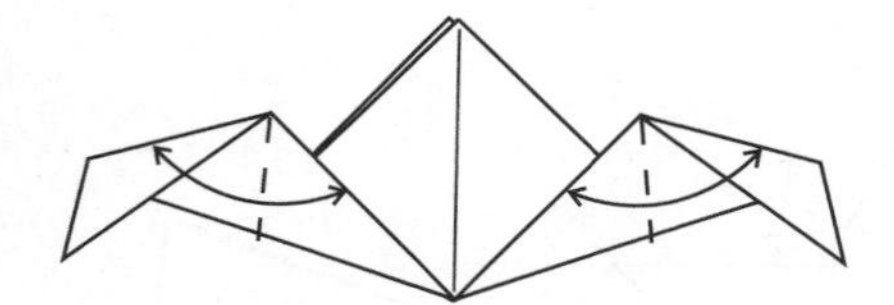

7. Fold and unfold each wing in half.

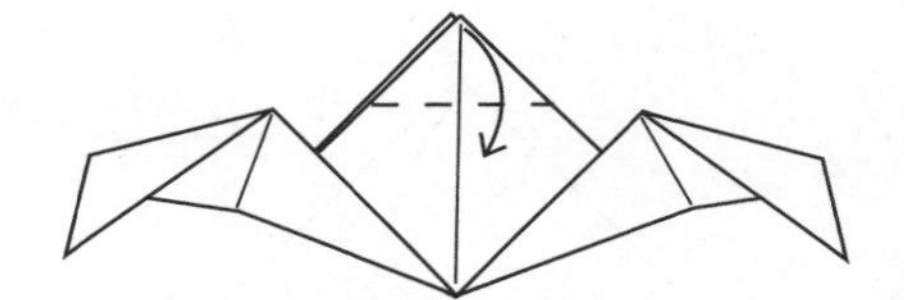

8. Fold down the top corner (both layers) to form the head.

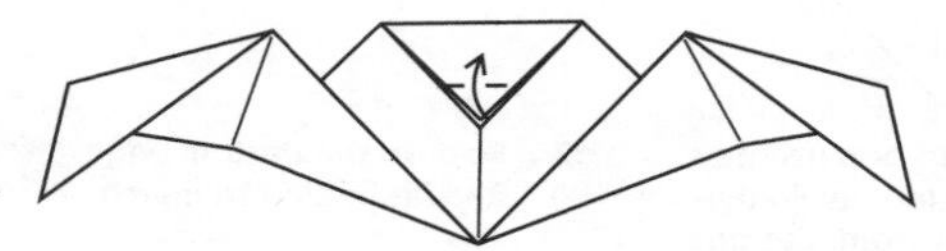

9. Fold up the corner (both layers) to make the upper lip.

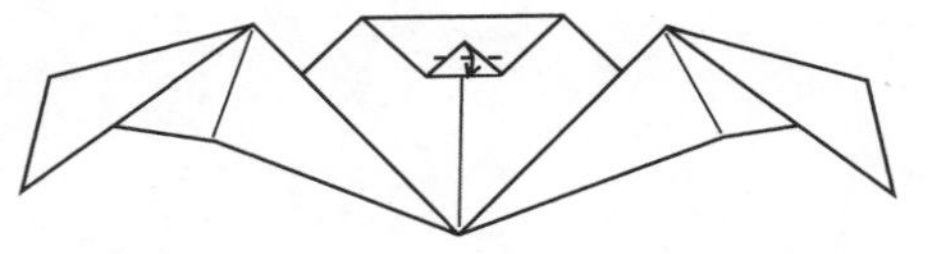

10. Fold down the corner (both layers) to make the nose.

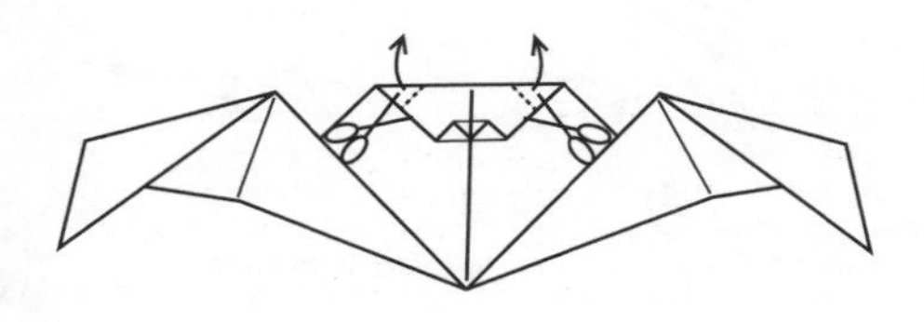

11. Cut on each side of the head. Fold up the ears.

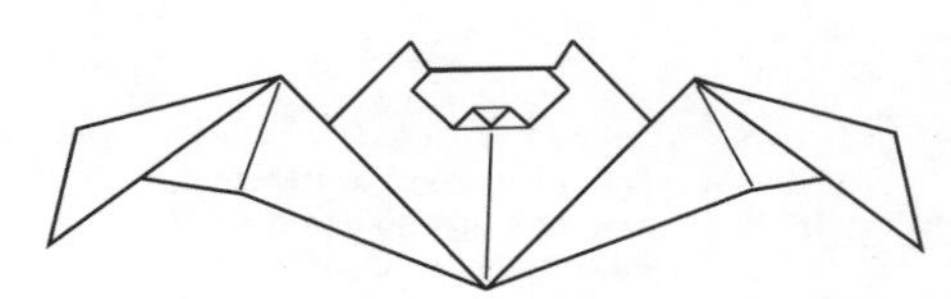

12. The finished Bat.

Swordfish

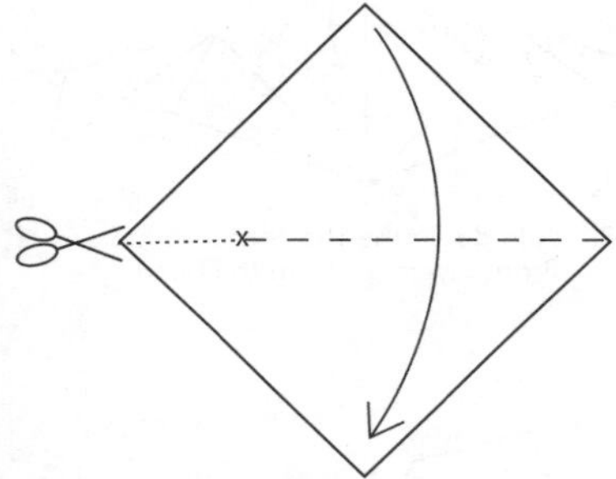

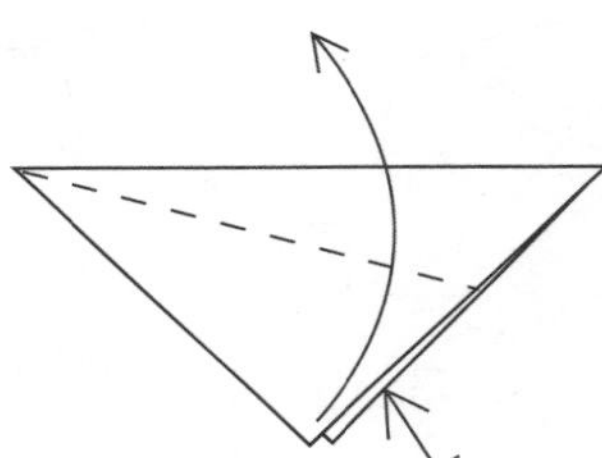

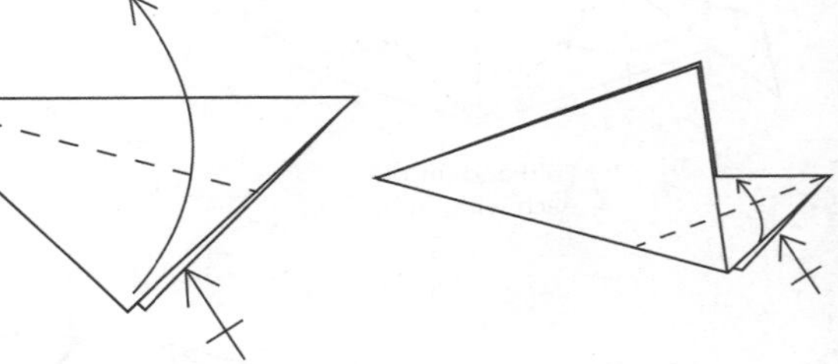

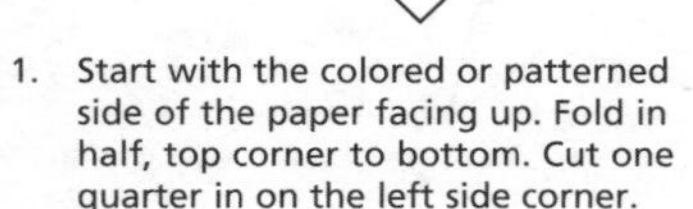

1. Start with the colored or patterned side of the paper facing up. Fold in half, top corner to bottom. Cut one quarter in on the left side corner.

2. Fold up the bottom edge. Repeat behind to match.

3. Your paper should look like this. Fold the bottom short edge up, matching the folded edge above it. Repeat behind.

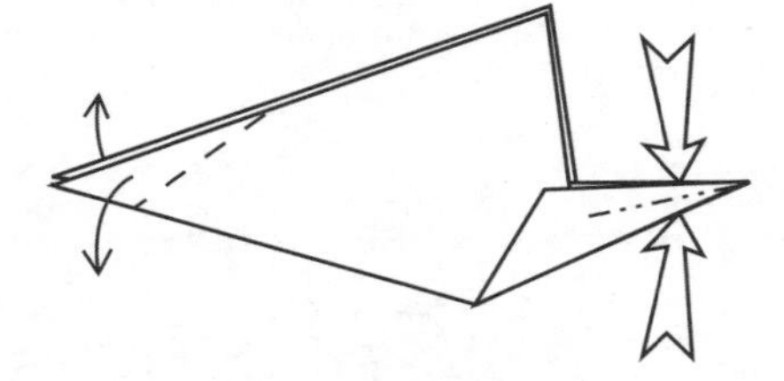

4. Fold the corners at the cut end, one up and one down. Pinch the nose spike flat.

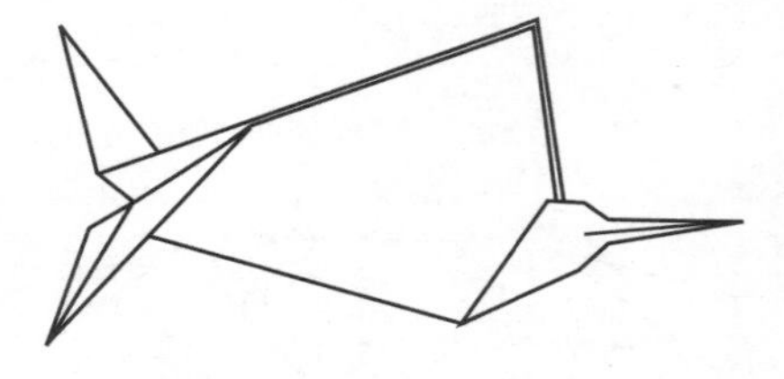

5. The finished Swordfish.

Seahorse

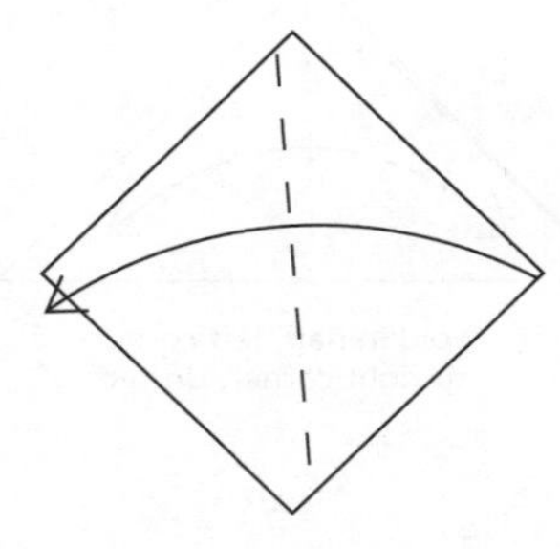

1. Start with the white side of the paper facing up. Fold in half. Do not match corners.

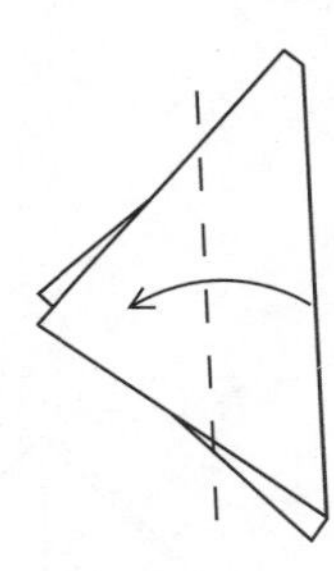

2. Fold over.

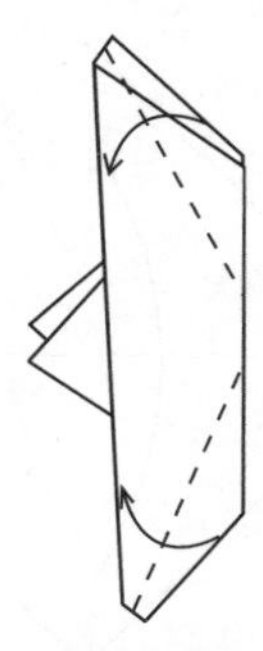

3. Fold the top and bottom edges to the common folded edge.

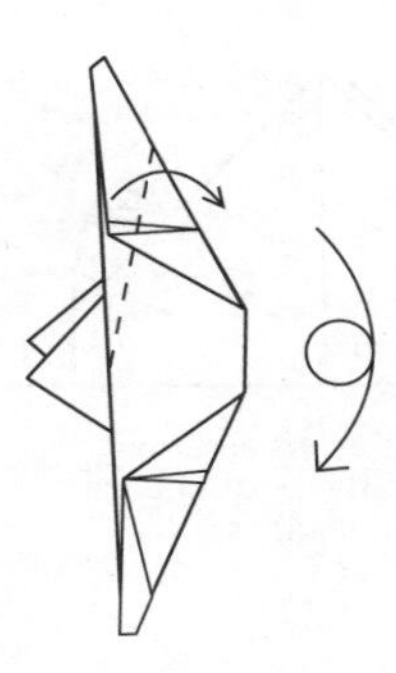

4. Fold top point over. Turn over, top to bottom.

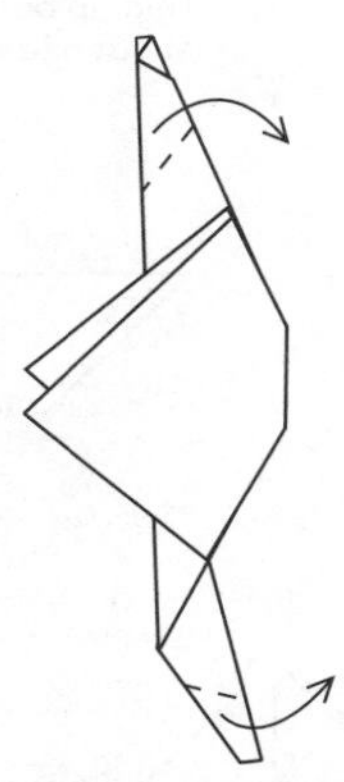

5. Fold down the top point to form the head. Fold up the bottom point for the tail.

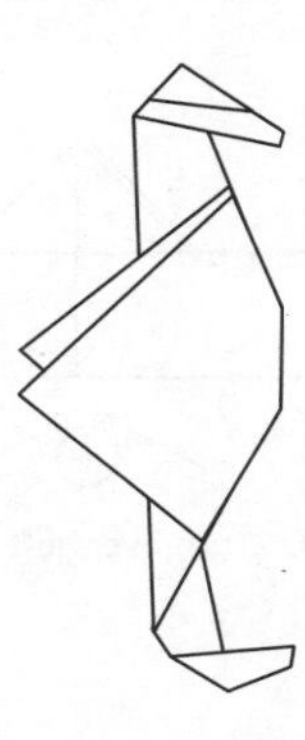

6. The finished Seahorse.

Bat

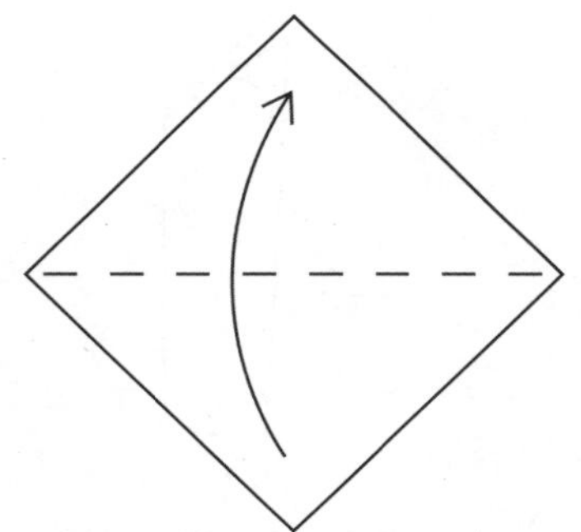

1. Start with the white side of the paper facing up. Fold in half, bottom corner to top corner.

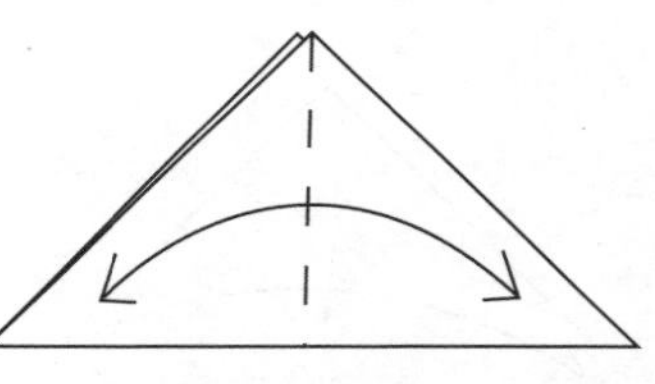

2. Fold in half, left corner to right corner. Unfold.

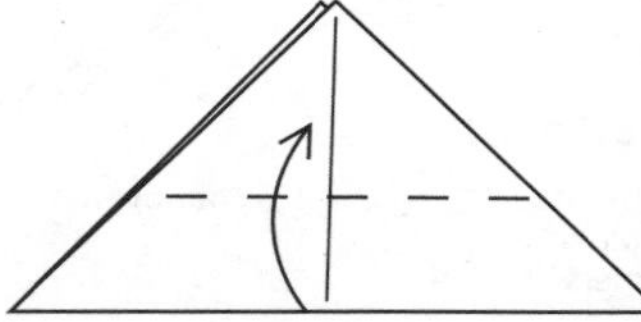

3. Fold up bottom edge, about one third.

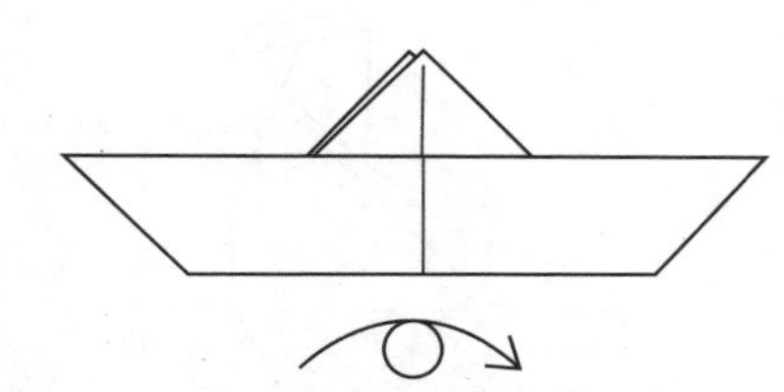

4. Turn over, left to right.

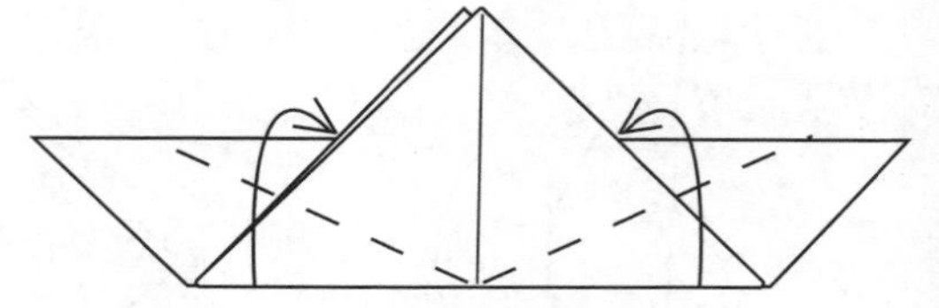

5. Fold up the left and right halves of the bottom edge to form the wings.

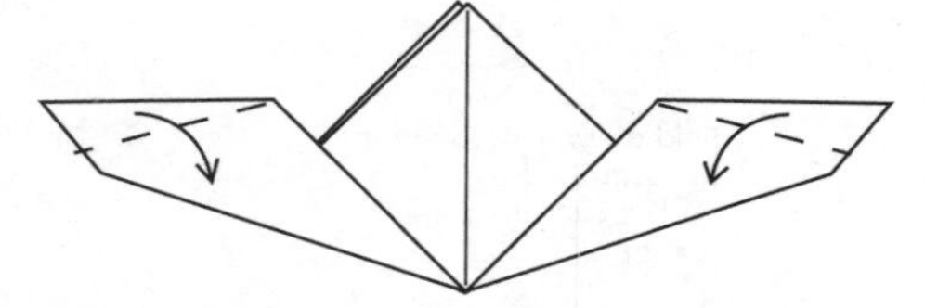

6. Fold down the outside corners of the wings.

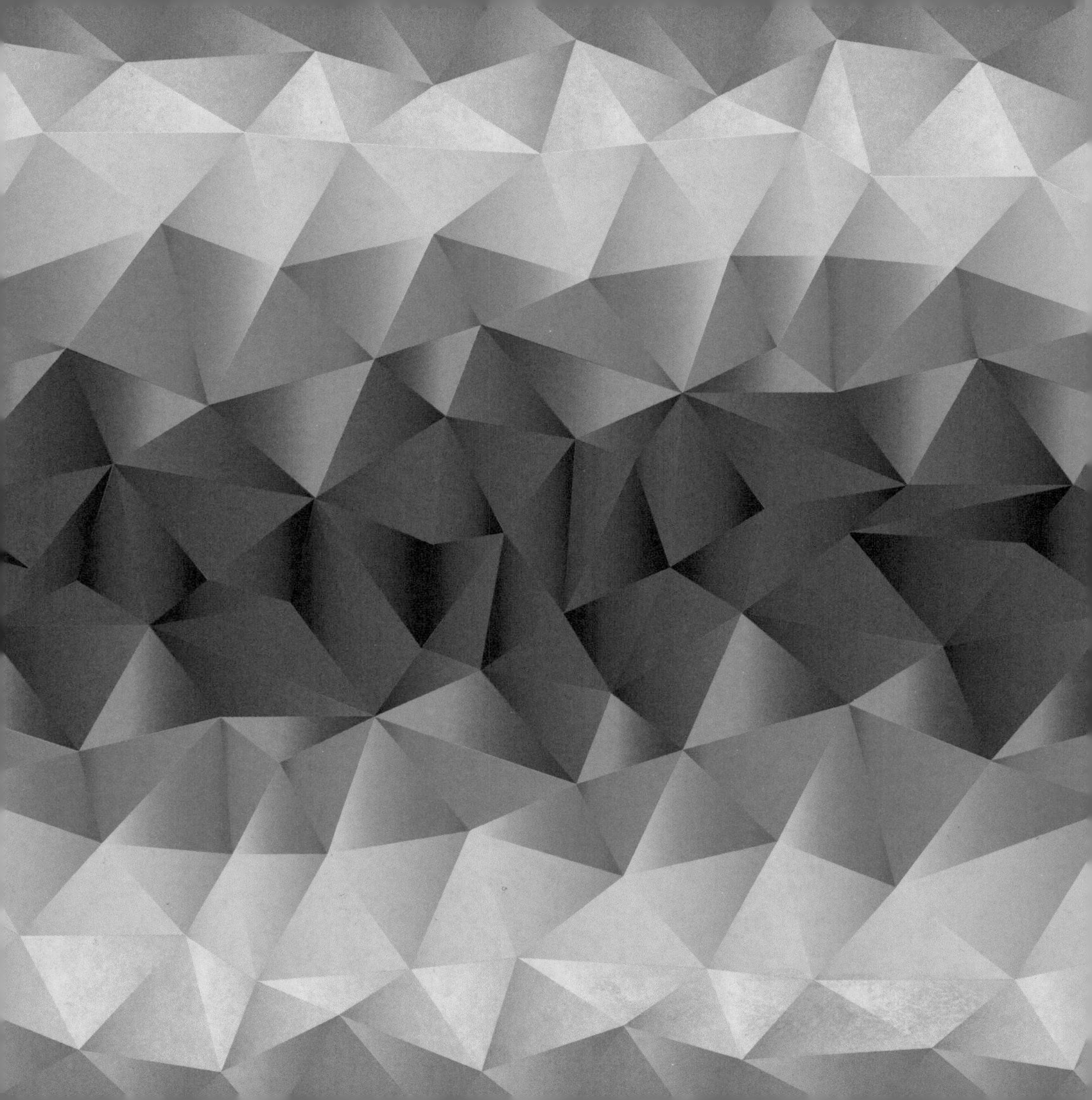

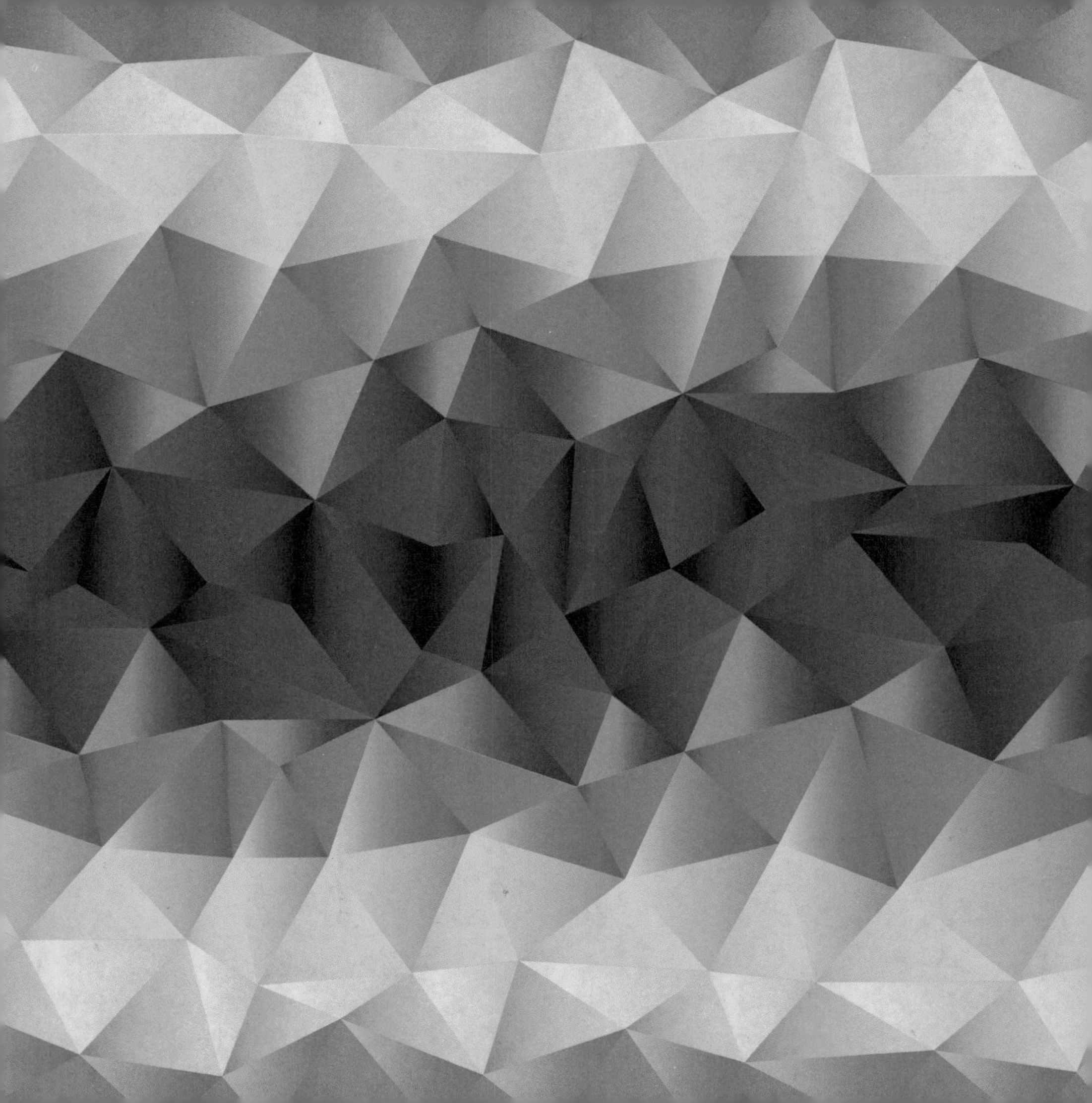